D1597623

SNOW DAY

ALSO BY DAWN QUIGLEY

Jo Jo Makoons:
The Used-to-Be Best Friend
Fancy Pants

DAWN QUIGLEY

SNOW DAY

ILLUSTRATED BY
TARA AUDIBERT

Heartdrum
An Imprint of HarperCollinsPublishers

Heartdrum is an imprint of HarperCollins Publishers.

Jo Jo Makoons: Snow Day
Text copyright © 2023 by Dawn Quigley
Illustrations copyright © 2023 by Tara Audibert

Library of Congress Control Number: 2023933192
ISBN 978-0-06-301543-2 (trade bdg.)
ISBN 978-0-06-301544-9 (pbk.)

Typography by Andrea Vandergrift
23 24 25 26 27 LBC 5 4 3 2 1

First Edition

To Gabrielle and Maria,
my favorite little snow bears
—DQ

To all Indigenous little girls who never got
to see themselves in storybooks
—TA

❧ ABOUT THIS STORY ❧

Jo Jo lives on a fictional Native American Ojibwe reservation, the Pembina Ojibwe Reservation. A reservation is land under the care of a Native Nation that calls it home. The land now called the United States is home to more than three hundred reservations and over five hundred Tribal Nations. There are many reservations in the United States, but Jo Jo's is not an actual one. Every reservation has unique and special elements, and Jo Jo's reservation incorporates many of those found in Ojibwe (and many other Native American) communities.

KOKUM

MIMI

MAMA

CHUCK

JO JO

FERN

PENNY

BRIE

SUSAN

FERRIS

TEACHER

CONTENTS

VitaMimi

"**M**imi, you need to eat your treat."
Mimi is not answering me. Or looking at me. *Again.*

"Remember, they help your teeth be nice and clean?"

Sometimes I do not like stinky kitty breath. Well, I do not like stinky kitty breath *ever.* It is not very fresh.

Sniff sniff. "Mimi, this smells so good! It is a very tiny kitty vitamin."

Hmm, Mama always says to be *helpful* to little ones.

"See, Mimi, look at me! I'll show you how yummy the vitamin is." But I just pretend to eat it because this medicine is not for human kids. Just cat kids.

Sometimes I wish I could take a vitamin that's just for kids. 'Cept Mama always says it's better to get my vitamins from the food I eat. Vitamins have letter names like the alphabet: B, C, and D. But I've never seen the alphabet of vitamins in my food.

Wait, I know! Alphabet soup must be *very* healthy! ABCs all into me!

Mama and my kokum always talk about being healthy. Kokum has something called die-beeties. She has to eat healthy all the time. But Kokum sneaks little things like cherry Life Savers when Mama isn't looking. Kokum is in love with sugar.

Kokum gives me a winky-blink when she

sneaks her treat. That means it's our little secret. But I want her to be a healthy grandma, so I say, "And tonight at dinner you will eat *extra* alphabet soup, my girl!"

My name is Jo Jo. You can call me Jo Jo. I am seven years old and in the first grade. My real big name is Josephine Makoons Azure. My middle name is Makoons. You say *Makoons* like this: ma-KOONS. It is a very good middle name because it means little bear cub. And my hungry tummy growls loud just like a little bear cub's, too!

But I will not bite you. I promise.

I live on the Pembina Ojibwe Nation. We speak Michif and Ojibwe and English. Michif is a language made from words that are Cree, French, and Ojibwe.

It is good to have many languages here because we talk a lot. Sometimes my Auntie Anne talks so much I stare at her stomach to make sure she remembers to suck in air.

My Elders say that we are citizens of this Ojibwe Nation. Teacher told us you get to vote if you're a citizen. But if *I'm* a citizen, when do I get to vote? I would vote for more Saturdays. And more ice cream. And less school.

I stand by the kitchen sink and watch until Mimi takes her kitty vitamin. It's the one that cures stinky kitty breath.

"Oh, good job, Mimi!"

Meooow.

Yay! Now I can take her into my blanket fort in my room to play rummage sale. I always play the cashier and Mimi is the shopper. Well, she's the only shopper, but she finds the best deals!

Mimi is just about to pay (she uses kitten kisses to pay) when Mama pops her head in our rummage-sale fort. "Jo Jo, do you have my measuring cups?"

"Well, hello, ma'am. Why, yes, we have a

lovely set right here," I say in my best cashier voice.

She puts her hand out. "Okay, I need them, my girl."

"Righty-o. That'll be twenty-five cents, please," I say, tilting my head. Tilting your head means you are being helpful.

"But they're mine."

"Eya, and for only twenty-five cents you can have them! We take cash or check, ma'am. Or cookies."

Mama looks at me and sighs. She must think it's a very good price!

After eating my cookie, I clean up my rummage sale and go to set the table for dinner. Setting the table means grown-ups want you to use your fancy manners. I learned all about being fancy from my Auntie Anne's wedding. Fancy manners are like not using your sleeve for a napkin, putting your pinky finger up when you write, swallowing your burps, and *not* spitting your peas in the milk to hide them. Although making green polka dot milk is very pretty.

"Mama, can Mimi sit with us at dinner tonight?"

"No, Jo Jo. Mimi is a cat, not a person."

"But, Mama, Mimi is family. You always say, 'family first,'" I say with fast blinking eyes. That means I am being very serious and full of truth.

Mama does not say anything (which means she did not say no!). She lip-points to Kokum's room.

"Okay, I'll go get her," I say.

I skip down to Kokum's room. Her door is open, and she is taking her medicine. Hmm, she is being very *healthy*. Our tribal chair is always reminding us to stay healthy in every season. Our Elders are very important, and it is good to check on them.

We hold hands and walk back to the kitchen (because Kokum's skip is a little slower lately).

Hmm, there are Mama's running shoes by the door. She is being very *healthy* when she runs. Sometimes when she leaves the house for a run, Kokum says, "Are you planning on coming back?" But she always says it with a giggle laugh. I love Kokum's giggle laugh. It sounds like a mermaid blowing bubbles.

Hmm, Kokum is being healthy, Mama is, too, and even Mimi was also being very healthy when she ate her kitty vitamin. And she only spit it out three times!

I want to be healthy, too! But I think I should try to be neighborly to make sure everyone is staying healthy. The tribal chair says we need to check on our neighbors to make sure they are okay. And very important to do it in the winter!

I will be a very neighborly neighbor. Even to Brie (who is *not* a best friend). Maybe. Or maybe not.

"Make way for the chef!" Mama says, bringing dishes to the table.

When grown-ups say *chef* it means they think they are very good cooks. Sometimes they are wrong.

We all sit down to eat. Mimi, too.

"Jo Jo, I said Mimi can't sit at the table."

"But she's not! She's sitting in my sweatshirt *hood*. See? She's *not* sitting at the table—she's sitting in my hood!"

Mama and Kokum look at each other quietly. For a long time. That means they're proud of me!

"Eya, family first!" I say.

Meeooooow.

Even Mimi agrees.

Jo Jo's Journal

Today is a school day. That means I have to leave Mimi at my house.

"Mimi, now be a good girl today, and listen to Kokum," I say, waving to Mimi on the way out the front door.

"At least that makes one of you," Kokum says on our walk to the bus stop.

Kokum's way of thinking is funny sometimes. But she is a very good kokum. And she is my very best friend. After Fern. And Mimi.

And even a better friend than my bear blanket. And . . .

Ferris, my bus friend, is saving my seat again. He even scrapes the frost off the windows for us in winter.

"Boozhoo, Ferris!" I say.

"Jo Jo, aaniin ezhi-ayaayan?" Ferris asks.

"I'm cold, but good! And I would be even more good if you gave me some of your donut."

He gives me a piece of the very delicious donut.

Ferris is a very good bus friend.

"Bus driver! Jo Jo is *eating* on the bus! Tell her that's not allowed!" Brie says.

Brie is *not* a good bus friend. That Brie has eyes all over. I bet she even has them in her very fluffy pigtails.

I peek out in the aisle and look at Brie. I chew my donut *very* slowly and lick my lips. And look and look at her.

She stares back at me. Staring means you agree! It *is* a very pleasant donut.

At school I walk past the office and right to the drinking fountain. That is where I meet my best friend Fern every morning! It is a very happy drinking fountain place. We hold hands and skip down to our classroom and through the door. Fern has not lost her quick skip.

Before we sit down, I help Fern hang up her jacket in our coatroom.

"Miigwech, Jo Jo," Fern says. Fern has a very quiet voice but a very big smile.

This month I sit at the yellow table. The yellow table is far away from Teacher's desk. It is the Teacher-just-needs-some-space-from-you place to sit.

Up-Chuck sits here, too. And Brie. Teacher needs some space from a lot of us.

"Class, today we will begin discussing a

very exciting topic, and one I know you will all like," Teacher says.

"Is it comic books? Comic books are very exciting, and we will all like them."

"No, and next time please put your hand up, Chuck," Teacher answers, but he looks at me when he says Up-Chuck's name.

Actually, Up-Chuck's real name is just Chuck. I call him that because he upchucked his lunch in kindergarten. Teacher doesn't like when I call him that (Up-Chuck always does a big belly laugh when I do). But then why does Teacher keep calling him that, too?

Teachers are confusing.

"No, children, today we will begin to study how to eat healthy foods. And how we can check in to make sure our Elders are healthy, too."

Our Elders teach us to eat more of our good Ojibwe food. I love to eat fish and wild rice! Wild rice is always very calm when I eat it.

Healthy food sometimes means grown-ups have to bribe you to eat it. But yay! Mama, Kokum, and Mimi are all healthy, so I want to be healthy, too.

"So let's all open our new Healthy Journals and begin filling in our answers," Teacher says.

Journals! I love journal notebooks! I have a fancy purple one with a unicorn. I wonder what this journal will look like.

Susan passes out the journals. They are blue. Blue is okay. But I hope there are glittery unicorns inside!

I hold the journal very softly and open it.

Guess what? It is not fancy. It does not have any unicorns. Or glitter. My eyes are very disappointed.

"Makwa, can you please read us the first page?" Teacher asks.

"Eya, page one: 'Let's all be healthy! Fill out the rest of the sentence and draw pictures to show how you know how to be healthy,'" Makwa reads. He is the best reader I know. After me. And Mimi.

Mama always says to give something a try before giving up. So I will try. I pick up my pencil to begin.

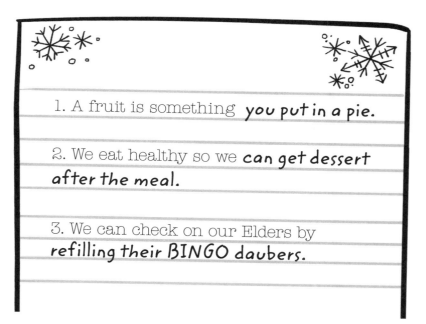

1. A fruit is something *you put in a pie.*

2. We eat healthy so we *can get dessert after the meal.*

3. We can check on our Elders by *refilling their BINGO daubers.*

Okay, maybe learning to be healthy will be fun! I will be very good at being *healthy*!

My Elders and neighbors will be so happy when I help them be healthy, too! It is very *neighborly* of me to do this.

Thirsty Grape

At lunch I sit between Fern and Susan. I never know what Mama will pack in my bag. Sometimes she packs a tuna-fish sandwich, which means she mixes up my lunch with Mimi's. Today it looks like I have crunchy nuggets in a baggie.

Hmm, is this Jo Jo food or Mimi food? It looks like Mimi's kibble cat food.

I look up at the ceiling, where I find many good ideas.

"Oh, who would like to try this?" I ask the kids at the table.

Joe says, "Eya, I will!"

I watch him eat it. Will he grow whiskers if it's Mimi's kibble?

"Mmmm, good granola, Jo Jo! Miigwech for sharing," Joe says.

Oh, it's not kibble! But it is good to let your friends taste-test first. It is healthy for *me*.

Whew. Oh, well, at least he didn't grow cat whiskers. It would not be a good look on him.

Back in our classroom I sit down at the yellow Teacher-just-needs-some-space-from-you table.

"Okay, children, let's put our math work away and begin sharing our Healthy Journal homework!" Teacher says with many enthusiasm.

I don't know what they teach at teacher school, but there must be a class on pretending to be excited about giving out homework. I bet Teacher got an A.

"Who would like to read their page-two work?" he asks.

Oh, I really think my answer is good. I shoot my hand up quickly. And use a pointy-finger tipi. Pointy-finger tipis are when you make a home with your fingers. That means your fingers know the answer.

Teacher calls on me. I read my journal page aloud and show my picture.

Raisins are *just very thirsty grapes*.

Teacher looks at me with 11 forehead. That 11 forehead means grown-ups scrunch their eyes together and make an 11 between their eyebrows. They are confused.

I wonder why grown-ups are confused so much. Must be because they stopped believing in unicorns.

"No, Jo Jo. The answer is 'Raisins are *a fruit*,'" Teacher says.

"But how do you *make* a raisin?" I ask.

"Well," Teacher answers, "water is taken from grapes to make raisins. They're dehydrated."

I look at Teacher. Then at the kids. "So, if raisins don't get water, wouldn't they be thirsty?" I ask, tilting my head. That means I am being *helpful*. I try to help Teacher every day. It is another way to be *neighborly*.

"*I'm* thirsty," Up-Chuck says.

"Me, too! I'm thirsty!" Susan says.

"Teacher, water is healthy, right?" I ask.

"I'm thirsty! Let's take a water break!" the class yells.

Teacher rolls his eyes. Rolling his eyes means he believes us that water is healthy! And that a raisin is a very thirsty grape.

"Line up, students. We'll take a water break," Teacher says with a *very* big, slow sigh. Yay, water!

It is so good to be healthy!

We get ready for the end of the day. It starts to snow at bus time! Yay, snow!

We all put our snow pants, boots, hats, and mittens on.

This means we are bundling up. Bundling also means you are hiding from the cold.

Snow means fun outside time. I hope there is enough snow to make snow bears on the

ground. My grandpa and I used to make snow bears. It is like making snow art about my middle name. Snow bears are very Makoons. Just like me!

Teacher walks us to our buses. He walks me to mine, looks at me, and says, "Goodbye, Jo Jo. I don't know how your family does it."

"Well, good thing I like to help them!"

Teacher looks very tired. Maybe he should take a nap. Naps always perk up Mimi and Kokum.

Mama tucks me in that night.

"Mama, will it keep snowing?" I ask.

"Well, yes, I think so. Right now, there is moisture in the air. If it's cold enough, the water droplets freeze into snow crystals."

I look out the window.

Hmm, everyone knows snow is when unicorns fly too close to clouds. They sneeze and it makes snow. Everyone knows that. But not Mama, I guess.

I think grown-ups learned too much and forget about how important unicorns are.

No Yellow Snow

Mama wakes me up early the next morning. Too early. Kokum says I am not a morning person.

My pillow drool is still wet. And clingy to my cheek.

I am a very good sleeper.

"Jo Jo," Mama whispers. "Today is a snow day. There is no school. It's canceled."

"What? But Teacher said they won't cancel school 'cause now we would go online."

"Jo Jo, all the snow and ice last night caused the reservation's internet to go down. It will be out for at least a day. I heard it on the tribal radio station just now. Now go back to bed, my girl." Mama kisses my bear-ear PJ hood.

No school! Oh my!

I did not know what a snow day was. I never had one last year in kindergarten.

A snow day must be when the teachers do not want to shovel their driveways to go to school.

Then they call the principal to tell her.

I have very much love for my teachers this morning. They must have hoped for a very lot of ice and snow!

"Mimi, let's get up! I'm too excited to sleep in!"

Meow.

Mimi gets up and moves to the end of my bed. Away from me and my excitement.

"Mimi, come on, my girl, let's play rummage sale! There will be lots of new things for sale 'cause Mama's not up. I happen to have a lovely new pair of running shoes you might like."

Rrrow.

I don't think Mimi is a morning kitty either.

I'm hungry for breakfast.

Hmm, I'm not allowed to pour a big milk container in my cereal bowl 'cause last time it rained milk all down the table.

Teacher says it's healthy to eat a good breakfast. I will make my own breakfast the Jo Jo way! (Yay, yay, for the Jo Jo way!)

Mama and Kokum always write down their special recipe. I will, too.

1. Check to make sure everyone is still asleep.

2. Wash hands with special soap for silky smooth hands.

3. Find bowl (NOT Mimi's dish).

4. Pick healthy cereal.

Hmm, Teacher says healthy foods are colorful foods.

5. Pick healthy cereal with the dinosaur-shaped fruity-ohs. And only add one spoon of sugar.

6. Look at the milk in the fridge and remember not to use it because I am not allowed.

Not allowed means grown-ups think you messed up before.

> 7. Find milk to put in very colorful dinosaur-shaped fruity-ohs.

I sit, tapping my head, looking at my un-milk breakfast. Tapping your head helps ideas come faster.

I know! What is *made* of milk?

> 7. ~~Find milk to~~ put ˄ice cream in very colorful dinosaur-shaped fruity-ohs. Watch it melt into delicious milky goodness.

Teacher is right! This healthy breakfast is *very* good!

* * *

Now, what do I do on a snow day?

First, I play dolls, and color, and arrange all the kitchen spoons by size and how nice they are to me. Next, I put little signs up around the house to remind everyone to be *healthy*.

It is good for me to be a *neighborly* neighbor at my house, too!

Feed Mimi kibble (not Jo Jo).

Use running shoes to run. Big sale on them at Jo Jo's rummage sale.

Cherry Life Savers do NOT save lives. (This is for Kokum.)

Then, I clean up my delicious, healthy breakfast. Kokum wakes and sees me cleaning it up and says, "Discarding the evidence, eh?"

Sometimes her way of thinking is funny.

But she always gives me very big hugs. Kokum's breath smells like cherry Life Savers. And pudding.

I hold her face and say, "Kokum, you really have to break up with sugar. It is not good for your die-beeties.

"Remember, Kokum, you always say to eat more of our good, healthy Ojibwe food! Like fish and wild blueberries? Even Mimi likes fish!"

She stares and stares at me. Staring at someone means you agree!

It is *neighborly* to remind my Elders to be healthy.

Later that morning Mama says, "Jo Jo, the snow has finally let up a bit. Why don't you get dressed and play outside?"

She looks at Kokum. Then at me. "You can take a break, Jo Jo."

Taking a break means grown-ups need some alone time.

Whew, maybe I do need a break! I have
been very busy on my snow day morning.

Mimi didn't want to play checkers, even
though I said she could pick which color she
wanted to be, so I decide to go play outside.

Put on snow stuff. Take off mittens to zip
up jacket. Why aren't zippers bigger for mit-
ten fingers?

I have very many thoughts about zippers.

Look at all the new snow outside to play in! It is beautiful. And fluffy. And glittery. And white. Marshmallow white.

It will be very important to remember what my bus friend, Ferris, told me last week.

"Jo Jo, remember not to eat yellow snow," he said with fast blinking. Fast blinking means he is very serious and full of truth.

Ferris is very good at helping me be *healthy*. And he was being so very *neighborly*, too!

It is good to be healthy, so I will sing a song to remember:

See, see the doggie pee pee?
Oh, don't eat the yellow snow, 'cause it's
  like icky pee tea.
I will tell you all to not eat the snowy
  pee pee.
I will even tell that to Brie Brie.

5

Zippers, Frybread, and Car Repairs

I start to make snow bears in the snow in the front yard. They are so pretty. And very Makoons!

Then I sing another little song. It is my very own made-up song!

Oh, snow day, snow day, what a very fun no-school day!

Hmm, what comes next?

*Oh, snow day, snow day, if you see yellow
    snow, just say, No way!*
*Oh, snow day, snow day, let's go find some
    other kids, okay?*

I am very good at songs!

But wait! I need to check on our Elders
and other neighbors. They need to be safe and
healthy, too!

I open the front door and ask, "Mama, can
I go to the neighbors to check on them?"

"Good idea, my girl. Here, I made some
soup and frybread. Please take it to them."

Kokum whispers, "And, Jo Jo, take some of
my cherry Life Savers to them, too."

I am very happy and kiss Mimi before I close the door. Extra kisses keep you warm.

Meeoow.

I take the bag with frybread and jars of soup with me out the door.

There are so many snowbanks to walk on. These banks don't have any money, though. Only snow. A lot of snow. But I have to check on our Elders!

I need to be healthy, too. Hmm. I am hungry again.

Wait! Frybread!

I only take a few *tiny* bites.

Nibble nibble. Tastes better than Mimi's kibble.

And a few more nibbles to make them circles. Circles are important.

Knock knock knock. Knock. Knockity-knock. Knock.

This knock means I am here with food!

I go to Mrs. Dette's house first. Because it

is next to me. And is the most pretty purple color. I think she must have unicorns living there.

"Oh, aaniin, Jo Jo! What are you doing here, my girl?" Mrs. Dette asks.

"Well, I'm checking on my Elders to make sure they are safe. Did you know we had a snowstorm?"

"Oh, eya, I did see that!"

"Mama sent this over." I hand her a soup jar. And a little frybread (that was a nice small little circle).

"Miigwech, my girl. Aren't you kind to check on me!"

Oh, I am being so *neighborly*! I will check on my other Elders, too.

I go to the next house. Mr. Mike fixed my bike tire last summer. I like to call him Mr. Mike Bike.

"Hello, Mr. Mike! I am checking on my Elders. And you are an Elder. Because you are older. Are you okay?"

"Eya, Jo Jo. That I am! Yes, my heat is good. Miigwech, my girl!"

Next stop is Auntie Shelly's house. It is a pretty pink house.

Auntie opens the door. "Oh, hello, Jo Jo! Why, what do you have here?"

"It is soup and a little frybread circle. I taste-tested it for you. I nibbled on the big piece to be sure it was healthy."

Auntie says, "Oh, well, miigwech, my girl. You sure are something."

Whew. I am very tired from being neighborly. Only one more to go.

Ms. Franny's house is the last one on my street.

"Aaniin, my girl, are you having a fun snow day?" she asks.

"Yes, Ms. Franny! The snow is so fun! How are you after this snowstorm?"

"Oh, my girl, I'm good! Warm and full. But . . . I'm worried about—"

Worried! Oh no! I have to check to make sure she is okay.

"I'm worried about the icicles that fell on my pretty red truck. They took some paint off."

"Oh, I'm so sorry! But I can fix it!"

I turn around and run to her truck in the yard.

Hmm, this is very reddie-red paint.

I know!

Rip, unwrap, suck, slurrrrp! Dribble spit.
There! All fixed!

Boy, Kokum's cherry Life Savers really *did* save the day!

Winner Olympics

"Mama, can I go across the street to the park now?" I ask, peeking in the front door. "I'm all done checking on the neighbors!"

"Eya, I see Ferris's moushoom over there watching the kids. But be sure to look both ways before crossing the street." Mama looks out the window and waves at Ferris's grandpa.

Crossing the street on a snow day means

you have to put your hands out to catch the snowflakes. It is good to help the snow cross the street.

"Aaniin, Jo Jo!" Ferris yells. "Are you staying away from the yellow stuff?"

Ferris's grandpa is sitting on a park bench. I wave at him.

All my friends are here playing in the snow! What fun! Even with Brie here. (Brie is *not* a best friend.)

I say we should all make snow bears on the playground. They do not agree.

"I am going to make a snow dancer in the snow. It is because I am the best dancer. Everyone says so," says Brie.

I move my eyes left and right *sideways*. Sideways means you do *not* believe someone.

"I'm going to make an up-Chuck chucker," Up-Chuck says, laughing. He makes a pile of snow with leaves and twigs spilling out. It is not very lovely.

Susan pats her pile into a long snow table. "It's my boss desk at the casino!" Susan wants to be the Bingo boss when she grows up.

All the kids do their own snow art. But there is only one snow bear—the one I make. "Hey, everyone," I say. "Let's do something together! This is how our tribe always does things."

Fern whispers in my ear. Hers is the smallest voice, but the smartest sound.

"Yes, Fern! Good idea! Teacher talks about being healthy. And we learned about the Olympics games from Jim! Let's do our own winner Olympics," I say, very full of energy.

"Jo Jo, our gym teacher's name is Mr. Morin, not Jim. And it's *winter*, not *winner* Olympics," Brie says, very full of sarcastic.

I put my hands over my mouth. That means I am trying not to yell back at Brie.

"Eya! This will be fun! We will be athletes, like Jim says," all the kids yell. Brie does not

yell with us. She is being what Kokum calls *sour.*

An athlete is someone who is healthy and gets to play for work.

Ferris says, "Let's all meet back here after lunch. My moushoom said he and my kokum will come watch us all."

All the kids, or, um, I mean, all the *athletes* go home to eat.

Tuna and Tears

"Mama, I'm home. Guess what we're going to do?" I ask. "We're going to make our own fun Olympics!"

"Athletes need food. So, wash up, Jo Jo, and sit down with us for lunch."

I sit at the table, so excited. What food will Mama give me to be healthy?

Mama makes me a sandwich. I peek under the bread.

It makes my tongue sad. And my eyes gloomy.

"Jo Jo, eat up your tuna sandwich and apple so you can get back outside to play," Mama says.

I need some time to think about this sandwich. The sandwich I *know* is supposed to be for Mimi.

I have very many feelings about it. So, I get out my Healthy Journal from my backpack. I fill out page 7:

Today I will eat **a tuna sandwich (that was for Mimi, I think).**

It will taste like **sadness. With a side of tears.**

I have to think very hard for the next one.

It will make me healthy and **give me very fluffy and shiny skin.**

This lunch will help me be an athlete, or a cat-lete.

Kokum sits down next to me. She lip-points for me to move over.

"Jo Jo, why aren't you eating? I heard you all having fun at the park. Don't you want to get back?"

"Kokum, why do grown-ups make us sad food?" I ask with very fast blinking eyes. This means I am being very serious and full of truth.

She looks at my lunch (the sad, stinky tuna-salad sandwich).

"Jo Jo, remember we Ojibwe eat our good, healthy food. I made that bread using wild rice."

"Okay, Kokum. I like our healthy Ojibwe food. But will the wild rice make me *more* wild?" I ask.

"I'd never call someone 'wild,' but it's fair to say you have a big personality," she answers.

"What sandwich is Mama making you?" I ask.

"It's a BLT, my girl," she answers.

Hmm, it's another alphabet meal, like alphabet soup. It must be healthy. I wonder what *BLT* means? I know: butter lemon toast. Yum!

"Kokum, I'll give some of my lunch to Mimi. And we can share your lunch! It's what we Ojibwe do. We share our food," I say, giving her my biggest gum smile. That means I am being nice.

Mama comes in carrying a plate. "Make way for the chef!"

I wonder why Kokum gives me a winky-blink. That means we have a secret joke.

After lunch I need to write in my Healthy Journal again. I have some new feelings.

Write about a <u>new</u> healthy food you tried.

Dear journal,

Today I tried a BLT sandwich. I will tell you something shocking. It is <u>not</u> a butter lemon toast sandwich.

There was bacon (that is the B). I like bacon. And it likes me, too! Kokum says it's because we're both salty.

But the L is for lettuce. Not lemon. Lettuce is okay, but it should mean "let-us not eat something very good."

The T is <u>not</u> for toast. It is tomato. A tomato tastes like an apple that gave up.

56

I am not sure about this healthy stuff anymore. But if it gives me a shiny coat, I will keep trying it!

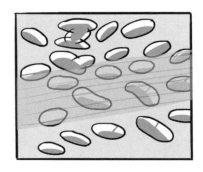

Let the Games Begin!

All the kids come back to the park. They look so very happy! I bet they didn't have tuna for lunch.

Kokum decides to walk me across the street. I guess the snowflakes will have to wait to cross the street. "Jo Jo, I'll go say hello to Ferris's grandparents. It's been a while since we visited."

I give her a very big Jo Jo hug and say, "Kokum, will you stay and watch our Pembina Olympics?"

"Eya, my girl." And she kisses my nose. That is how some Elders say they love you.

I snow-skip to the big hill in the middle of the park. It is where all the kids are playing. It's the tallest hill on the reservation. And it is right across the street from me!

It is very lucky to live so close to me.

"Jo Jo, so what will our Olympic games be?" Susan asks.

Brie yells, "Why does Jo Jo get to decide? She doesn't even know it's called winter games, not *winner*!"

Brie is what Teacher calls *interesting*. It is interesting that she always thinks she's right. Nobody is always right. Right?

Joe says, "Well, Brie, I guess because she came up with the idea."

"Yeah," Up-Chuck says. "Ideas are really hard."

I reach out and tap Up-Chuck's head *gently*. I'm trying to help him have ideas. Tapping your head makes you think faster.

But I don't think it is working for him.

Fern reminds us that we need to have a lot of games for our Olympics.

All the kids start yelling game ideas.

"I know, let's have a skiing race."

"No, let's have a skating game!"

"How about sledding?"

Fern clears her throat. That means she is going to say something. Something important.

We all stop talking and look at her.

"But we need to make our Olympics our *Ojibwe* games. Because we are on our Pembina lands," Fern says.

Fern's ideas are so very good! And very Ojibwe!

All of us huddle to talk about our ideas. We even let Brie in our circle. (Fern said we had to.)

This will be so fun! And healthy!

We all run home to get some things for our Ojibwe Olympics.

"Let's meet back here in a few minutes!" I yell.

Heart Healthy

Kokum walks me back home and to the park again. Her smile is so big. And she is humming. She must like snow days, too.

All the kids run to the big hill to start our parade for the games.

It is very good to be healthy during our Olympics start. And we need a bright torchlight.

First, we rolled down the hill to see who would be last. It was such a good game!

Next, we use Makwa's mama's burned frybread. She was going to throw it out, but we use it in our games!

It is good to recycle to keep the neighborhood clean. I am good at being *neighborly*!

More Elders and neighbors come to the park when they hear us having fun. All us kids get in a circle and listen to Fern's new idea.

"Eya!" we yell.

Fern walks back to the whole group and says, "The next Olympic games are for *everyone*."

We each take an Elder's hand and walk them to the starting line.

"Jo Jo, you know I can't run anymore," Kokum says to me.

Fern answers, "Oh, this is a game for everyone. That is what we do. All are welcome."

She looks at Penny and nods. Penny has a

very nice loud voice. She has what grown-ups call "strong lungs."

"Ready, set, go!" Penny yells.

And that starts the Ojibwe Olympic lip-pointing race!

Ferris's grandpa wins! He had the longest lip point! I think it must be a new record.

"Okay, everyone back down the hill. Hold hands in a circle. It's round-dance time!" Penny yells. It is good her lungs are so strong!

Up-Chuck's uncle brought his hand drum and starts to sing.

Holding hands, we all move our feet slowly and dance to the left.

"Jo Jo, my girl, you . . . you are so . . . ," Kokum says with wet eyes. The snow must bother her eyes.

What a fun time! It starts to get dark out, so we close our Olympics.

Everyone has a very full heart. And very big smiles.

Hmm, maybe there are many ways to be healthy?

We walk back home. Kokum's footsteps are lighter and faster. Kokum found her skip.

The next day at school we all tell Teacher about our Ojibwe Olympics.

"It was so fun!"

"Children," Teacher says, "that sounds wonderful. And you were being so healthy! Oh, I used to love snow days back when I was young."

When grown-ups talk about being young, you have to pretend to be interested in "the olden days." But it's okay to listen to their stories. Sometimes we learn important things (like there was a time *before* TV!).

"We had lots of games!"

Teacher continues, "Oh, did you play King of the Mountain?"

We all look at him. I tilt my head (which means I am being very helpful). "No, Teacher, we are Ojibwe. We don't have a king."

Susan says, "We played Tribal Chair of the Hill. Just like in our own reservation! We all climbed up, and they had to help us get to the top."

Teacher nods. "Oh, yes, well, children, you must have made a fort with snow walls?"

Brie says, "No, why would we make a fort with walls? Who are we keeping out?"

Sometimes that Brie is okay. (Just sometimes.)

"We made a big snow wigwam. Big enough for all of us to sit in!" Up-Chuck says. It was very nice of him to turn his snow Up-Chucker into a wigwam.

Teacher listens to all of the other Olympic games we played. He just stares at us. He blinks his eyes very many times. And keeps wiping them. It must be his allergies?

"Well, very good, children. Please open up to the last page of your Healthy Journal and work on it."

I tap my head to help get good ideas.

Dear journal,
Vegetables are never going to taste good.
Might as well put sugar on them.

Cherry Life Savers saved the day. But I
will try real fruity fruit cherries. I bet they
will be even better!

Fruit is the next item to have at my big
rummage sale! Yay, fruit!

Being healthy also means being together.
I will even bring our good Ojibwe wild rice
to school. It is neighborly and healthy to
let Teacher eat our food.

I learned to be *healthy* by being *neighborly* with my neighbors in the winter. Yay for our snow day!

It is so good to be healthy!

JO JO'S GLOSSARY

A glossary is a very fancy word for a small dictionary. It is where you can learn about new words and how to say them. These are some Ojibwe and Michif words from this story:

aaniin (AH-neen): hello, greetings

aaniin ezhi-ayaayan? (AH-neen ayzhi-u-YA-yun): How are you?

boozhoo (BOO-zhoo): hello, greetings

eya (ee-YEH): yes

kokum (KUH-kum): Michif word for grandma

makoons (ma-KOONS): little bear cub

miigwech (mee-GWECH): thank you

moushoom (MUH-shoom): Michif word for grandpa

AUTHOR'S NOTE

The Ojibwe people belong to many Bands (or groups) and Nations. I am part of the Pembina Band of Ojibwe. My reservation is the Turtle Mountain Reservation in North Dakota. It is the current land for the Turtle Mountain Band of Ojibwe.

The Ojibwe Nations are within the borders of the United States and Canada. Some of our Ojibwe reservations are within the borders of North Dakota, Wisconsin, Minnesota, and Michigan. Just like Jo Jo said, we speak Ojibwe, but also many other dialects, or versions, of it. My Turtle Mountain reservation uses Ojibwe and Michif.

Dear Reader,

Jo Jo knows that it's important to be neighborly, and I bet you do, too!

How are you neighborly? Do you watch out for little ones or check on your Elders or share your lunch or have fun playing with your friends on snow days?

Could you be more neighborly? For example, you could plant a little garden and share vegetables you grow. That would be neighborly and help others to be healthy, too.

Being neighborly—showing that you care—is healthy for everyone. To have healthy hearts and minds, we all need to be kind to each other and to accept kindness.

Have you read any other stories about Jo Jo Makoons or other Ojibwe heroes? How about characters from other Indigenous Nations? I hope this book encourages you to read more.

Jo Jo Makoons: Snow Day is written by Dawn Quigley, illustrated by Tara Audibert, and published by Heartdrum, a Native-focused imprint of HarperCollins Children's Books. An imprint is like a little umbrella under the bigger umbrella of a publishing company. We publish stories by Native writers and artists about Native heroes who are kids like you.

Maybe you could share this book with a fellow reader! That would be neighborly and a healthy way to spend your time. Be sure to look for more books in the Jo Jo Makoons series!

Thank you for reading,
Cynthia Leitich Smith

DAWN QUIGLEY is a citizen of the Turtle Mountain Band of Ojibwe, North Dakota. Both her first book about Jo Jo Makoons, *Jo Jo Makoons: The Used-to-Be Best Friend*, and her debut YA novel, *Apple in the Middle*, were awarded American Indian Youth Literature Honors. She is a PhD education university faculty member and a former K–12 reading and English teacher, as well as Indian Education program codirector. You can find her online at dawnquigley.com.

TARA AUDIBERT is a multidisciplinary artist, filmmaker, cartoonist, animator, and podcaster. She owns and runs Moxy Fox Studio, where she creates her award-winning works, including the animated short film *The Importance of Dreaming*, comics *This Place: 150 Years Retold* and *Lost Innocence*, and "Nitap: Legends of the First Nations," an animated storytelling app. She is of Wolastoqey/French heritage and resides in Sunny Corner, New Brunswick, Canada. You can find her online at moxyfox.ca.

CYNTHIA LEITICH SMITH is the bestselling, acclaimed author of books for all ages, including *Rain Is Not My Indian Name*, *Indian Shoes*, *Jingle Dancer*, *Hearts Unbroken*, and *Sisters of the Neversea*. She is also the editor of the anthology *Ancestor Approved*. Smith is the author-curator of Heartdrum, a Native-focused imprint at HarperCollins Children's Books, and is the Katherine Paterson Endowed Chair at Vermont College of Fine Arts. She is a citizen of the Muscogee (Creek) Nation and lives in Austin, Texas. You can visit her online at cynthialeitichsmith.com.

In 2014, **WE NEED DIVERSE BOOKS** (WNDB) began as a simple hashtag on Twitter. The social media campaign soon grew into a 501(c)(3) nonprofit with a team that spans the globe. WNDB is supported by a network of writers, illustrators, agents, editors, teachers, librarians, and book lovers, all united under the same goal—to create a world where every child can see themselves in the pages of a book. You can learn more about WNDB programs at www.diversebooks.org.

More books about
Jo Jo Makoons!

DAWN QUIGLEY

Jo Jo Makoons

THE USED-TO-BE BEST FRIEND

ILLUSTRATED BY TARA AUDIBERT

DAWN QUIGLEY

Jo Jo Makoons

FANCY PANTS

ILLUSTRATED BY TARA AUDIBERT